The Christmas Puppy

A Polly Parrett Pet-Sitter Cozy Murder Mystery

Liz Dodwell

Liz Dodwell

The Christmas Puppy: A Polly Parrett Pet-Sitter Cozy Murder
Mystery: Book 5
Copyright © 2016 by Liz Dodwell
www.lizdodwell.com

Published by Mix Books, LLC

Joy to the World

Table of Contents

One

"Tom, as soon as the Mayor finishes his speech the lights will come on. That's your cue to drive round to the front of the house."

"So what time should I be out there?" Tom Ouelette looked at Rooster. "Do we even know how long the Mayor will talk?"

Rooster shrugged and turned to Mom. "Any thoughts, Edwina?"

Mom shook her head while she backed her chair away from the desk and wheeled herself across the room where she could face us all.

"Mayor Dinkins is scheduled to speak at six-forty-five – it will be quite dark by then - and has been given a suggested time of no more than 10 minutes. Unfortunately, he does tend to like the sound of his own voice so expect him to go on for 20. If he exceeds that we may have to implement plan B."

"What's plan B?" Diego spoke up.

"Rooster could suddenly have problems with the sound system." Mom winked and we all laughed.

It was the final meeting of the Welcome Home Christmas Festival committee. It was also Thanksgiving morning and we were all in great good humor, looking forward to a grand dinner with all our residents and then to the Grand Opening of our Christmas Festival the following evening.

I should explain, Welcome Home is the place my mom and I established to provide housing for homeless military veterans and their pets. The property is made up of the farmhouse – our old family home – a couple of converted barns, and various other outbuildings. We had the capacity to house 17 residents, and we were full. We didn't have medical facilities or anything like that; I suppose you could say we were more of a halfway house. Our goal was to provide a temporary home until the vets could re-establish themselves back into a normal life. And, very importantly, we welcomed pets.

It's amazing how many veterans and other homeless people will refuse to enter shelters because their best friends are not allowed. We're trying to change that. And here in Maine, where the winters are long and very cold, we didn't want anyone or their pets to suffer without shelter.

I tuned back in to the conversation, where we were tweaking the details of our annual Christmas Open House. This was our third year and, with the help of all the residents, it was going to be a doozy.

"Polly!"

"Uh, yes Mom."

"I hope you're ready with the dogs."

Just because I have a pet-sitting business everyone seems to assume I can train animals to do anything. I mean, I can teach a dog to sit, stay and roll over – most of the time

8

– but getting them to perform in a pageant is a totally different thing. None-the-less, I'd been designated to come up with an act to include at the Opening, and when my mother tells you you're going to do something well, let's just say there's no point in arguing.

"Yep, we're good to go," I lied.

"What are you going to do?" It was Tom, our designated Santa who asked.

"The dogs will be dressed as elves and working in Santa's toy shop. Except Angel," she's my pit bull mix, "who is playing the part of Rudolf." That's if I could get her to keep the red nose and antlers on.

"Are they going to make toys?" grinned Carl, a marine combat veteran who'd served in Vietnam.

I gave an airy wave of my hand and replied vaguely, "That will be a surprise," because based on my lack of success in our "rehearsals" what happened on stage was likely to be as big a surprise to me as it was to anyone else.

We talked a little longer, discussing refreshments, the raffle, other entertainment, 'til Rooster called a halt and gave a quick summation.

"Tom, you will get into your Santa suit and be out back at least 15 minutes before the Mayor begins speaking at six-forty-five. The packages will have been loaded into the carts and the train ready to go by six-thirty. Carl will be out there to help you until then, but if you're late you'll be on your own because Carl," Rooster cocked a finger at the man, "you'll have to hustle to the stage and make sure the choir is in position behind the curtain."

Some of the guys had built a little trolley train in which Santa was going to make his appearance, driving out of the trees to the front of the house. It would be pulling a couple of carts filled with packages that we were going to raffle. Oh, I should have told you, the aim of the event was to raise money for Welcome Home; running a shelter was a very expensive business and we relied heavily on the kindness of our community. The event was also designed to showcase what we were doing and, perhaps most importantly, spread the joy of the season to one and all. I know that sounds sappy, but that's how we all felt.

Rooster pointed at Diego, who had been with the Army Corps of Engineers as an interior electrician. "You'll need to be running a final check on the Christmas lights. We don't want any problems when the Mayor flicks the switch to turn them on."

Glancing at his notes Rooster continued. "Back to you, Carl. As soon as the mayor finishes, the curtains will open and that will cue your music.

"Tyler," Rooster said to my boyfriend who, so far, had been very quiet, "you're in charge of props, so be sure everything is ready."

"Yes sir," Tyler gave a mock salute, then blew a kiss my way. I caught it and pressed it to my lips and there was a general groan amongst the others and murmurings of "Yuk," and "Get a room." We just grinned at each other.

"OK, everyone," Rooster called the meeting back to order. "We're nearly done. Edwina," he addressed Mom, "you'll be at the food booth with Scott and Lou. Hayley," she's our only female resident, "is in charge of selling raffle tickets. The Mayor will finish speaking and turn on the lights, Santa will appear driving the train as the choir sings. We'll have about an hour for folk to buy tickets and food, kids to sit on Santa's lap, and for everyone to admire the display. Polly, you and I will be floaters, helping out wherever needed, just give yourself time to get ready for your own entrance on stage. The pageant will begin promptly at eight. Are we all clear?"

There was a chorus of "Yes" before everyone gathered up their notes and hurried away.

My nose drew me straight to the kitchen where Scott Hamm and Lou Berger were prepping for the Thanksgiving dinner. There would be more than 20 of us sitting down to eat, so tables had been pushed together in the bigger of our two dormer barns as we could no longer fit everyone into the house.

"It smells absolutely wonderful in here. Any chance you're in need of a taste tester?"

Scott rolled his eyes at me as Mom wheeled her way in behind me. "The only way you get to stay here is if you pitch in and help," she said.

"Anything." I held my hands palms out. "I'll even peel potatoes as long as we can listen to Christmas music."

"Deal," Lou said. He pulled an ipod from his apron pocket and in moments we were listening to Rockin' Around the Christmas Tree.

"Alright," I said, "just hand me the peeler and I'll get cracking."

"Actually, Polly," Scott looked over his shoulder from the range where he was stirring something in a big pot, "I'm about ready to fill the pie crusts. Would you grab them from the pantry? I set six of them in there to cool."

"Sure thing." I rocked my way across the kitchen floor, singing along with Brenda Lee (she's the one who first recorded the song, in case you didn't know) and opened the pantry door.

The people who built these old farm homes understood the importance of a pantry, and ours was huge. Right now, it was also packed with jars of jams and relishes that Lou and Scott had prepared to sell at our event, along with the usual stuff Mom kept in there. I gazed around looking for the pie crusts. *Ah!* Of course they were on the highest shelf. Not to worry, though, we kept a small step ladder handy. It was a bit shaky but it did the job. I climbed to the top, still bopping around to the music.

Oh, no!

You're thinking I fell, aren't you? Well, for once I wasn't a klutz. No, I was looking at the six pie shells, neatly lined up to cool, and in one of them my little orange and white cat, Amber, was curled up fast asleep.

"How did you get in here?" I hissed, lifting her from the shell. She wriggled and swatted at me, annoyed to be taken from her warm, cozy bed. I shoved her inside my sweater and tucked the sweater into my jeans. I looked as if I was about to give birth to some strange alien life form, but I knew Amber would soon settle down and go back to sleep.

Pulling the pie shell from the shelf I studied the hairs lining the inside. Tentatively I blew on them. Several of them rose lazily into the air then drifted down onto boxes of pasta and rice. *Oops.* That wouldn't go over well with Mom.

I tried picking the hairs out one by one, but it was really hard to see them. *I know, I know.* You're grossing out now, but I didn't want to be the one responsible for messing up Thanksgiving dessert and having to beg everyone's forgiveness. *Maybe if I shook the shell?*

Flipping the pie dish over I gave it a quick shake and, for good measure, a hearty slap on the bottom, which is when the shell slipped out and fell to the floor in a crumpled heap.

"What on earth are you doing?"

Mom was in the doorway. Startled, I nearly did tumble off the steps but saved myself by grabbing at a handle. It gave me enough leverage to find my balance and jump to the floor. Unfortunately, the handle was attached to a drawer that came with me, spilling its contents of neatly folded aprons and kitchen towels beside me. Under my sweater Amber dug her claws into my stomach in an effort to hang on, and growled in protest at the jerky ride. I sucked in a harsh breath of pain.

"Hi, Mom."

My mother did what she usually does in these situations: looked Heavenward and probably said a silent prayer. Lou came rushing in when he heard the kerfuffle, closely followed by Scott. They tried extremely hard not to laugh too hard as I endeavored to explain myself. Nobly, I took the blame for everything on myself so Amber wouldn't be in trouble. Mom pointed out that Amber was my responsibility and I should have made sure she was kept away from the kitchen, so *of course* I *was* to blame.

Anyway, in the end I was banished from the kitchen while the other pie shells were examined for evidence of sleeping cats, and new shells were baked. The good thing was the story provided for much laughter at dinner; the meal, including all the pies, was delicious and by the time I was heading for bed I'd got over feeling like a scolded child and was very thankful for it.

Two

The puppy waddled into the clearing on chubby little legs. At eight weeks old he was quite fearless, but he was also tired and getting cold. He had no concept of time, of course, and didn't know he'd only been away from his mother for about half an hour. Still, darkness had now descended and the temperature was below 40F and dropping rapidly.

It was the lights at the back of the farmhouse that had drawn him there and he was happy to see a human sitting in a box thing. Obviously, he couldn't understand it was Santa sitting in the train, but humans were nice to him, they picked him up and cuddled him, and he was ready for some serious snuggling.

He broke into an unsteady jog, his ears bouncing up and down as he went. At the train he skidded to a stop and yipped for attention. *Hmm.* The human apparently didn't hear him so he tried to jump into the train, but his stocky body wasn't built for athletics and he plopped back on the ground. He yipped again. Still no response.

Undeterred, the pup tried again and again, and at last was able to hook one of his back legs over the running board. Scrabbling furiously he hauled himself aboard. Pleased with his success he swatted at the human's leg, making gurgly growling noises and whining. This behavior, he'd learned very quickly, always elicited immediate sympathy from humans and he would be picked up and talked to in that sing-song voice that made him feel warm and happy.

It wasn't working! What was wrong? The puppy had never been ignored like this before. He redoubled his efforts and bounced up and down, trying to claw his way onto the human's lap; all to no avail.

Puzzled that he was being ignored, the pup sat on the floor and looked up into the human's face. Not that he could actually see the face, because it was so hairy. He shivered, and awareness of being cold began to make him quite cross. He gathered himself for another leap, his little butt wiggled and he launched himself upward.

He almost made it. His front paws latched onto the seat and he tried to claw his way up. As he did so, one back paw hit a little switch tucked under the seat. It didn't even register in his brain but, in fact, the puppy had just put the vehicle in gear. Then he lost his tentative hold and tumbled backwards onto the foot pedal. All he knew was that something gave way beneath him and the train jerked, then he rolled to the side. That jerk was enough to cause the human to slump forward and his knee to come down on the pedal, holding it there, and the train began to move.

The puppy didn't budge. He didn't want to, because the folds of Santa's coat had fallen over him and at last there was something to keep him warm.

Three

Mayor Dinkins was five minutes into his speech when I felt someone tugging at my arm and twisted around to look into the anxious face of Dorcas Phipps.

"Polly, Mule has gone," she said.

I must have missed something in the planning because I had no recollection of a mule being involved. And why would Dorcas, the head of a local bulldog rescue group, have anything to do with a mule?

Reading my confusion, Dorcas hurriedly explained.

"Mule is one of the puppies. So many people have been looking at them and picking them up, I lost track. Mule is a stubborn little guy - you probably guessed that already from his name - and I should have been more careful. It's just like him to go exploring if he got the chance, but I'm scared. We've got to find him soon; he'll never survive the night and it's already dark."

Dorcas's words were beginning to run together and tears were welling in her eyes. Mule was one of five puppies born to a bulldog, Charlotte, owned by a well-meaning but decidedly stupid pet owner who thought she could mate her female and just leave the dog to get on with giving birth.

A little research would have taught her that the puppies' large heads can make whelping difficult, and sometimes a C-section is necessary. This was one of those cases, and by the time the owner realized there was a major problem and got the dog to a vet, it was too late for two of the puppies and Charlotte nearly died.

Traumatized by what had happened, the woman gave her dog up to Dorcas in whose care the mother had recovered and the pups were thriving. To introduce the one male and two female puppies to potential adopters, Dorcas had asked if she could bring the family to our Open House. She'd set up a tent with heating and had welcomed a steady stream of admirers, but now another one of the pups was in danger of his life.

It took me only a few moments to process the situation and decide immediate action was called for.

"I'm going to interrupt the mayor and start a search. Probably half the people here are ex-military and they know how to handle an emergency."

I made to push my way through the crowd to get to the stage when I became aware of a stirring in the people behind me. A young voice cried out, "It's Santa," while an older voice immediately followed with "Watch out!"

Standing on tiptoe I peered over the heads to see Tom in the train, heading for the crowds. It registered almost simultaneously that he was too early, was going in the wrong direction and was slumped over. I bolted toward him, yelling out "Move! Let me through!" The crowd milled in confusion and one guy roughly pushed me aside so that I almost fell. Recovering, I pressed on and caught a glimpse of someone else rushing in from the opposite direction.

It was Rooster. He got to the train first, reached in and flipped the switch. The train came to an abrupt halt, Santa wobbled then flopped to the side and a high-pitched wail came from beneath him. Rooster bent and pulled off the Santa hat as I bent and lifted his cloak.

"It's not Tom," Rooster said.

"Mule!" I cried.

"Hey, that's my Santa suit." I swiveled my head to see who had shouted. A figure was stalking in our direction. It was Tom.

Four

"His name is Chandler Slattery, he's a real estate developer."

Officer Wayde Frellick stood in the living room and addressed us - "Us" being Mom, Rooster, Tyler and me - as he gave up the identity of the dead man, and we all gasped.

"But he's the man who wanted to buy us out," Mom said.

"Buy you out? You mean he wanted to take over your charity?"

"Hardly," Tyler sneered. "He approached me months ago to act as his representative and make an offer to buy the Welcome Home property, but there was nothing altruistic about it. He wanted to put in a single-family home development. I turned him down flat and told him Edwina and Polly would never consider it."

"And that's exactly what we did tell him when he came to us directly," Mom said. "He got very pushy, very rude, so I told him to leave and never come back."

I chuckled. "Actually, what you said was 'Don't you get ugly with me, you jo-jeezly dub.'" (For those who don't know, that translates loosely as "Don't you get nasty with me, you overblown idiot.").

"That's beside the point," Mom picked up again. "We didn't hear any more from him and forgot about it. Besides, we had other things on our minds. It was when we were having trouble with that nasty little man from the VA."

"What trouble would that be?" Frellick asked.

"Oh, he was giving us a hard time about the barn conversions. Made us jump through hoops to get them licensed for use as living quarters for veterans."

"You know, I think I saw him here," Rooster suddenly said.

"Saw who?" I swiveled to face Rooster. "Ward Nesmith?"

Rooster nodded.

"What the heck would he be doing here?" I wondered.

"He should be ashamed to show his face," Mom said.

"This Ward Nesmith," Frellick interrupted, "he's the one from the VA?"

"He was the inspector assigned to oversee the construction on the barns," Rooster said. "But I can't be certain it was him. Coulda been someone who looked like him."

"OK, that's enough!" Frellick held his hand up in a "stop" gesture. "You can explain all this later. Meanwhile, the Sheriff wants you to stay put until he's ready to talk to you himself."

Mom wheeled herself practically toe to toe with the officer and pinned him with a flinty gaze.

"You're telling me Sheriff Wisniewski wants to keep me incarcerated in my own home?"

Frellick shuffled awkwardly. "Uh, no ma'am, he's requesting you remain here and not impede his investigation..."

"Impede his investigation?" Mom's voice was getting a little shrill. The rest of us knew the warning signs, but poor Frellick was out of his depth.

"Impede his investigation?" Mom repeated. "A man has been killed on *my* property. Our Open House has been shut down, which means a lot of people have been disappointed, our fund-raising efforts have been sunk and who knows how it will affect our reputation? A lot of good people who have served their country well, and then been abandoned by it, are relying on the Welcome Home organization for help, and you're telling me to butt out!"

"Well, I, I didn't exactly mean to put it that way."

"And what's more," Mom went on relentlessly, "there's a killer who may still be here. What are you doing about that?"

Frellick was saved at that moment when the door opened and there was Sheriff Wisniewski. He looked around the room, taking stock of the situation before directly speaking to Mom.

"We're conducting a murder investigation, and based on past experience," he looked pointedly at me, "I deemed it wise that we have a cautionary little chat about not interfering with police business."

Of all the nerve. I'd been caught up in a murder mystery or four in the past, but that didn't make me a liability. In fact, I think it safe to say my "interfering" had helped solve those crimes. Still, I crossed my arms and parked myself on the edge of one of the easy chairs and waited to see what else Wisniewski had to say.

"Reinforcements are on the way from County. There are a lot of people to interview and I'd like to set up in one of your barns so we can get people out of the cold while they wait."

Mom nodded assent then asked, "And what about us?"

"Frellick here will take your preliminary statements. I'll talk to you myself when I can."

With that he turned on his heel and walked smartly away.

We all looked at Frellick. "Well?" I said.

"I, uh, I'll need to talk to you each separately." No-one moved or spoke. "And privately," he added.

It was Rooster who took pity on him. "Come on. I'll go first. We can use the den."

"I need to let the dogs out," I said. My three – Angel, Vinny and Coco – were in a bedroom upstairs with Erik, the setter Mom had taken in recently, and Rooster's old pit bull, Elaine.

"You can't leave until I've got your statement," Frellick said.

"Don't be ridiculous. I'm not leaving town, I just want to give the dogs a breather. They've been shut up for hours now."

"You'll get me in trouble."

As always, it was Rooster who poured oil on the troubled waters.

"Don't worry, officer. When we're done, I'll bring the others to you," and he clapped a hand on the man's shoulder and guided him away.

"I'll come give you a hand with the dogs," Tyler said to me.

"Before you go..." Mom narrowed her eyes at us and jerked her head at the door. "Shut that."

Tyler stepped around me and pushed it firmly closed. "What's on your mind, Edwina?"

She took in a deep breath through her nose then exhaled loudly from her mouth. "I can hardly believe I'm saying this, but I don't care what the Sheriff says, I want us to do some investigating of our own."

My jaw went slack and I actually didn't know what to say. It's true in the past Mom had been in favor of leaving things to the authorities, so it was hard to accept her change of heart.

"Sheriff Wisniewski is a good man, and a good policeman...as far as it goes." Tyler and I exchanged bewildered glances at Mom's words. "But he's not a great investigator. He lacks imagination, and that's something that you, Polly, have in abundance.

"I meant what I said earlier; people are relying on us. The longer it takes to resolve this murder, the more it could damage everything we've worked so hard to achieve. What if this somehow jeopardizes our standing with the VA? We don't need funds being denied again."

We'd been through a rough patch not so long ago, when Veteran's Affairs had denied assistance to the Welcome Home residents. It had taken months to resolve and been very costly. I'd been so looking forward to this Christmas because we'd finally be able to put it all behind us. Now this!

"You've got my support," Tyler emphasized his words with a nod. "Do you have a game plan?"

"Well, I think we need to talk to Tom first. Or should we start by pooling whatever information we already have? You two are the ones with experience in this sort of thing. What do you think?"

"I think we'd better start writing things down," I said, "before we forget them. Let's each make notes of our own and have Rooster do the same, then we'll compare. After that, we can decide who else we should talk to."

"That makes sense. I'll get started while I wait for Frellick to come back. And Polly," Mom directed a stern look my way, "I want your promise that you won't go off on your own and do something silly."

I returned her look with a "Who, me?" one of my own.

"Polly..."

"Oh, alright, Mom. I promise."

"Tyler," Mom wasn't finished yet, "I expect you to make sure she keeps that promise."

He grimaced, "I'll do the best I can."

"I guess that will have to do," Mom said. "Go on and see to the dogs, then. We'll get together later."

Five

Tyler and I had to put the dogs on leads, which did not please them, but with much of the area around the house roped off, and cops everywhere, we didn't dare let them run loose. Welcome Home was on a little over 10 acres of land, so we walked as far from the hubbub as we could, only to discover some of our residents had had the same idea, including Scott and Lou.

"Hi, guys," one of the men greeted us. "Any idea how long this is going to take?" He gestured with his arm to take in the scene at the house, and in an instant questions were being thrown at us by everyone. I threw up my hands in mock surrender.

"Whoa, there. Give me room to breathe and I'll fill you in." And I told as much as I knew.

"What's the story with Tom?" The guy who asked was called Gerry. I couldn't remember his last name but I knew he was an ex-Army Corporal and his dog was called Andie, after a bomb-sniffing dog who'd saved his life in Iraq, then later lost her own.

"Yeah, what gives?" Scott queried. "Tom wouldn't hurt anyone but I saw him being taken away. We ought to do something about it."

"Was he in handcuffs?" Tyler asked.

"No, but a couple cops put him in the back of a cruiser and drove away."

Tyler and I looked at each other. The concern of the men was palpable, so much so it was affecting the dogs. Andie, who was a German shepherd mix, sat leaning against Gerry's leg and nosed at his hand for reassurance.

"Shall we?" Tyler asked me in a low voice.

I gave a brief nod of assent and turned to the men.

"Guys! Listen up! We agree something needs to be done, and so does my mom. Here's the thing, the Sheriff has already warned us not to interfere, but I promise you we won't let Tom take the fall for something he didn't do. For now, though, I'm going to ask you to hang tight 'til we have a better grasp of the situation."

"What does the Old Man say?" It was Gerry, again, and "Old Man" was the name the vets gave to Rooster, who was looked upon as a commander of sorts in our little community and was highly respected.

"He's being interviewed now, so we haven't had a chance to talk, which is all the more reason to be patient."

"Polly's right." Scott spoke up. "Let's see what the morning brings. You'll keep us up-to-date, right?"

"Me or Rooster," I said.

Tyler gripped my arm. "We'd better get back in case Frellick is looking for us."

I nodded agreement and again assured the others they wouldn't be left out, then we hurried away.

As we approached the house we saw a group of people outside the big barn. Voices were raised, though we couldn't make out what was being said, but it was apparent tensions were high.

"We'd better find out what's going on," I said, and veered toward them.

"Quiet down," I heard as I neared and realized the speaker was one of the county police who'd been called in to help. Not that anyone paid any attention to him, they just kept talking at once.

"Hey," I called out.

Either no-one heard or I was deliberately being ignored. I looked to Tyler for help and quickly he pulled out his phone and tapped the screen and a loud siren blasted out. It shut everyone up in an instant as I gave Tyler a questioning look.

"It's an anti-theft alarm," he said, returning the phone to his pocket.

"Polly, thank goodness you're here." Dorcas Phipps stepped from the group. "It's Mule. He's disappeared again." And she burst into tears.

Six

Softly, in the background, Pentatonix were singing "It's the most wonderful time of the year," which definitely didn't reflect the mood in the room. It was three in the morning and Sheriff Wisniewski was on a tirade.

"I should lock you all up. A man has been murdered and you lead a horde of people on a search for a dog!"

I gave him a sullen look. "A puppy. A very small and helpless puppy."

"Dog. Puppy. It makes no difference. You trampled all over a crime scene and probably destroyed vital evidence. And for what? Nothing!"

Next to me Dorcas began to sniffle and I rubbed her back; it was true, there had been no sign of Mule.

Mom, Tyler and Rooster were in the room with us but none of us responded to the Sheriff, we were too depressed to bother.

Wisniewski paced up and down as he ranted on, but all I heard was "blah, blah, blah." My mind was on the events of the evening, trying to make some sense of what happened. It wasn't working, I just kept coming up with more questions.

At last the Sheriff stopped moving and I realized he'd said something to me. "Uh...I, uh..." I fumbled for something to say.

"Is that clear?" Wisniewski snarled at me.

"Oh, absolutely," I said, hoping I looked as though I knew what he'd been talking about.

He held my gaze and I could feel my face heating up. *Stay cool, Polly.* It was only when he finally looked away that I realized I'd been holding my breath.

"OK, now that I've got your attention," the Sheriff ran a hand through his hair, "I have a couple of questions. There's a headless garden gnome on your back porch. What can you tell me about it?"

Huh? I pulled a face at Tyler, in return he gave me a helpless shrug. Then Rooster spoke.

"A couple of the residents got hold of some old gnomes and decided to repaint them as Christmas elves. One of them got dropped and the head broke off." He looked around at us. "They're concrete," he added, then turned his attention back to the Sheriff. "You'll see several of them out front as part of the display."

"You said 'headless gnome,'" Tyler frowned. "Does that mean you can't find the head? What's the significance of that?"

"It's the murder weapon," I said with dawning realization. "Chandler Slattery had his head bashed in by a gnome – in a manner of speaking."

"As usual you're jumping to conclusions Miss Parrett. I didn't say anything about how the victim was killed."

"You didn't have to, I was there, remember? So were Rooster and Tom; when Rooster took off the Santa hat we all saw the man's head was bashed in and bloody. If he was hit first and the hat put on him later, there will be blood all over the gnome's head."

I heard Dorcas moan and glanced at her. She looked awfully pale. I guess she wasn't used to murders like the rest of us. Still, I prattled on.

"If you didn't find the head perhaps the killer took it with him to get rid of later. He might have thought his fingerprints were on it." A thought struck me. "Had the head been painted? Surely you can't get fingerprints off concrete, but a heavy coat or two of paint would be a different story. The smart thing, of course, would be for the killer to have crushed the head and completely obliterate any evidence."

The Sheriff's hand smacked down on the old mirrored sideboard against the wall that had originally belonged to my grandparents.

"What part of 'absolutely' did you mean when I asked if you were clear about keeping your nose out of this?"

So that's what he'd been saying.

"Sorry, Sheriff. I tend to have an active imagination." I threw a furtive glance at Mom and saw a corner of her mouth turn up. "It won't happen again."

He drew himself up tall. "Make sure it doesn't. Now, can anyone tell me if you know of any relationship between the deceased Mr. Slattery, and Ward Nesmith who works for the Veterans Administration?"

Well, this was unexpected.

There was complete silence and blank looks.

"What sort of relationship?" Mom asked.

"Do you know if they were acquainted? Did any of you see them talking before Mr. Slattery's body was found?"

My jaw dropped. "You were right, Rooster. Nesmith was here."

Wisniewski pinned his sights on Rooster. "You saw the man?"

"I *think* I did," Rooster affirmed.

"Come with me!" Wisniewski commanded. To the rest of us he said, "You can all leave now. I'll deal with you in the morning, so be sure you can make yourselves available."

Tyler and I stood, Dorcas remained limp in the chair.

I crouched in front of her. "There's nothing more we can do for Mule tonight. I promise as soon as it's light we'll get search parties going again. Don't give up hope yet."

Her look was forlorn but she pushed herself to her feet. "I know you'll do your best Polly, I just…" Her lip trembled and the words were lost.

Mom wheeled herself over. "Dorcas, perhaps Tyler could drive you home," Tyler gave a brief nod. "Get some rest and come back in the morning."

"If you don't mind, I think I'd rather stay. My van is a camper, so I can be comfortable in there with Charlotte and her other two pups."

"We can do better than that," Mom was emphatic. "You can stay in the house."

"That's sweet of you, but I'd rather be in the van. The dogs are used to it and maybe a miracle will happen and Mule will find us there."

I forced my features to stay blank, not wanting to show my thoughts that a miracle was all Mule had left.

"Let me walk you out." Tyler took Dorcas's arm and she leaned heavily on him. I noticed Tyler brace himself. Dorcas was a big woman; not fat, but big-boned and tall.

I moved to the window, pulling back the drapes and peering into the dismal dark, thinking how much I'd been looking forward to the lights, the laughter, the good cheer.

"It's so depressing." I turned back to Mom and crossed my arms.

"Do you remember," Mom said, "when you and your brothers were quite small we had a chimney fire shortly before Christmas, and you were so worried that Santa wouldn't be able to bring your present because he couldn't get down the chimney?"

"Yeah, I do." In my mind I saw the four-year-old me struggling to stay awake to see Santa when he landed on the roof. I was planning to open the window for him to climb in, but things didn't work out as expected.

"We were never sure exactly what happened, but when your dad went to check on you before we went to bed, he found you hanging halfway out the window. It was 20 degrees and you were ice cold."

"I thought I heard reindeer on the roof. I was looking up to see Santa; I don't know what happened then."

"Well, something else you didn't know was the Pound Puppy toy you wanted so badly hadn't arrived in the mail. We didn't have the money, or the time, to order you another one. Of course, that didn't matter when we had to rush you to the hospital in Corkeep.

"We sat by your bed all night and all morning, with your brothers, and prayed you'd be alright. It was just about noon when you woke up, and the first thing you asked was…"

"Did Santa come?" I said. "And he did! He arrived right then."

Mom laughed. "He walked right to your bedside. 'Polly Parrett,' he said, 'I've been looking for you. I have a special present with your name on it because you've been a good little girl.' And he handed you a box…"

"It had paper with angels on it. I remember," I interrupted again. "It was my Pound Puppy. But, you know, I've never known who that Santa was."

"It was old Mr. Gregory, the post master. Your toy came in on a late Christmas Eve delivery. Mr. Gregory decided to bring it over himself on Christmas day, after he played Santa at the children's hospital in Corkeep. He hadn't known we were there but the nurses told him. His wife had wrapped the toy and he came looking for you after he said goodbye to the other kids. The timing was perfect, and you had no idea how close you came to missing Christmas altogether.

"But the point I'm making," Mom continued, "is that we prayed for a miracle and we got one. You were thrilled to meet Santa, and Dad and I were thankful you survived with no long-term problems."

"I'm not so sure about the long-term problems," Tyler quipped as he leaned against the door frame. I grabbed a cushion, which he ducked handily. "It was a good story, though, especially the bit about miracles."

"And now it's time we all got some rest," Mom said. "We need to be bright-eyed and bushy-tailed in the morning. We have a murderer to catch."

Seven

"Order! Let's have some order." Rooster stood on a makeshift dais of wooden pallets that we'd stacked in the horse barn. We'd lifted Mom up in her chair beside him. It was the morning after the ill-fated Open House. We were tired and tension was palpable among all who were present, which was about a dozen of the Welcome Home residents, plus Mom, Rooster and me. The other few had been deployed to run interference if any of the police – there were a couple still here – came near the barn. This was a secret meeting to jump start our murder investigation.

Military training tends to stick with a person and, instinctively, our veterans turned their attention to Rooster.

"You've all given statements to the police, but we don't have access to those, of course, so we're gonna ask you to repeat what you said, then maybe we'll have a round table – even though you're all standing in straight lines," there were a few chuckles here, "and see if we can make some sense of what happened. First, though, Edwina wants to say a few words."

Mom let her gaze roam over the group. "Rooster called you together because I insisted, so I think I owe it to you to explain my thinking. We all have a vested interest in Welcome Home, and every day the Sheriff keeps the lights turned off costs us money in lost donations. There's also a concern that we'll come under scrutiny from the VA again. But it's more than that.

"Christmas was when it all started. When Rooster and Elaine came into our lives." She caught hold of my arm and shook it gently, and smiled up at Rooster. I smiled too. "It was Christmas two years ago when the idea of Welcome Home was born. At that time we had nothing but the farmhouse, a couple of old barns and absolutely no money. What we did have in abundance was the heart to open our home, to give whatever comfort and encouragement we could, to men and women who had given so much to us, to our country, and then been forgotten or turned away when they needed help.

"You might say we were filled with the spirit of Christmas and I would agree with you, for I truly believe as the bible says, it's a time of great joy for **all** people. And Christmas reminds me how making that decision has brought me more joy than I can ever explain. Just look at what we've accomplished – together.

"I know it's trite to say we're all family, but no matter where you end up in this world, and what you may think of your time here, I want you to know you are always family to me, and you will always be welcome home."

Cheers erupted from those gathered and I heard calls of "Love you." Mom swallowed hard and snatched a tissue from the bag she hangs on the arm of her chair, and blew her nose loudly. When she regained her voice she went on.

"In a convoluted sort of way, I'm trying to tell you why Christmas means so much to me, and why it's so important to find Chandler Slattery's killer so we can get back to celebrating the wonderful things about this time of year. And rather than having a round table," she gave Rooster an apologetic look, "I think it would be most helpful if you would each write down your movements and anything you saw or heard, and hand it to one of us. After we've gone through them, we'll talk to you individually if need be."

"That's it," Rooster called out. "Find a quiet corner and start writing. When you're done, come over to the house and we'll chat."

"Just a minute!" I waved my hands above my head. "Mule, the bulldog puppy, still has not been found. Would you please all keep an eye out for him? It's possible he found a place to shelter and is still alive."

Almost all our residents had a pet, most of them dogs, and understood the risk to a small pup. They would also never give up looking, even though the odds were very much against Mule.

Tyler put his arm across my shoulders and gave a squeeze. "Just keep praying for a miracle," he said.

Eight

I bit the head off my gingerbread man. Some people start at the hands or arms and eat the head last, but it always seems a bit macabre to me to see the little fellow's smiling face as I devour his extremities and body.

"You know," Tyler said, "you could lick his facial features off. That would accomplish the same thing." (He knows my little idiosyncrasies).

I merely grunted. Not that it mattered right now. I could have stuffed the whole thing in my mouth at once and not enjoyed it much; I was too frustrated.

The two of us, with Mom, had been going through the resident's notes, but we weren't getting very far. There were no great revelations, nobody had confessed and no obvious answers to the mystery.

"Let's start with what we know," Mom said. "For one thing, the train was out back all day; I could see it from the kitchen window. I saw the trolleys being loaded up and Diego worked on something for a while, but nothing looked at all suspicious."

"I don't think any of that matters," I said, "unless you saw someone put the body in the train and hit the starter."

"I'd drawn the drapes long before there was a chance of that happening. From about four o' clock on anyone could have done anything and I wouldn't know."

"It's also conceivable that Mule somehow hit the starter and the body shifted on to the peddle," Tyler said.

"Do you think someone put the puppy in the train?" Mom asked.

I shrugged. "No idea. I can't imagine someone who's just murdered a man taking the time to rescue a puppy."

"You would," Tyler gave me a meaningful look.

I scowled at him. "So you think I'm capable of murder?"

"If someone was going to do cruel and terrible things to a helpless pet, or old person, or small child…"

I thought about that for a few moments. *Yeah, he was probably right.*

"Enough of that," Mom chided. She'd been sifting through the notes and pulled out a couple of pieces of paper. "Based on these," she waved the papers in the air, "no-one saw Tom after he'd helped Scott and Lou finish setting up the food table. That was around five-thirty. He told them he had to get into his Santa costume."

"Which he didn't." Tyler stroked his chin. "And that begs the question of where he was and what was he doing from that time until we discovered Slattery in the train."

"By the way," I said, "who had access to the Santa costume?"

Mom exhaled loudly. "Anyone who used the bathroom by the back door. That's where Tom was going to change. I hung the suit in there first thing in the morning and I'm sure at least a few people went in, but I couldn't say who."

"Hmm. We should probably ask if anyone noticed who used those facilities."

"That's really a longshot." Tyler reached past me to grab a gingerbread man. "Edwina, you said you couldn't see anything from four on. But Carl was out back later than that. So that narrows the window of opportunity for the killer from six-thirty to what? Six-fifty or so when the train appeared?"

"Ah," Mom shuffled papers again. "Carl was called away 10 minutes early, some confusion about sheet music, so the window widens from six-twenty to six-fifty, about half an hour. Plenty of time to do mischief."

"We really need to talk to Tom," I grumbled.

"With luck we'll be able to soon."

Tyler and I gave Mom a surprised look.

"Rooster talked to the Sheriff earlier. Tom hasn't been charged with anything and they're letting him go. Rooster's on the way to pick him up."

"Yes!" I raised a fist in the air. "What did he say? Why did they keep him so long?"

"Calm down, Polly. We'll find out when he gets here. Meanwhile, let's get back to what we know."

It was at that moment a couple of large dogs started barking to the tune, "We Wish You a Merry Christmas," while a chorus of small dogs and cats provided back-up. I pulled out my phone and saw it was one of my sitters.

"What's up, Jenn?"

"Oh, Polly, something's wrong with Little Bit. He hasn't had a bowel movement since I got here yesterday and he's been throwing up. You can tell he's very uncomfortable. I'm on my way to the vet, figured I'd better let you know."

"Good thinking, Jenn. I'll meet you there as soon as I can. Did you call Miss Teasdale yet?"

"No."

"Then I will. You've got your hands full already. You're doing the right thing."

"Everything alright?" Tyler asked.

"Cat emergency," I said. "I've got to run."

"Good luck," I heard as I dashed to my van.

Constipation is not unusual in cats, especially as they get older, but it can have lots of causes, some of them serious. And when the kitty is also throwing up and is in fact quite young – Little Bit, I knew, was five - a trip to the vet is the best course of action, especially when the cat is not your own.

Ardith Teasdale is an exceedingly sensible woman, I'm happy to say, and one who doesn't take chances with her pet's care. She was away for a few days on business but readily agreed her darling Little Bit should get whatever treatment Dr. Jim, our local veterinarian, recommended, cost be damned. So it was with a modicum of relief I arrived at the vet's office.

"Hi, Polly," the receptionist said. *They know me well here.* "They're in room three; just go on back."

I found Jenn with the doctor, looking over some x-rays.

"There you are," Dr. Jim gave me a nod of greeting. "I was just explaining to Jenn…"

My sitter began to speak at the same time. "He has to have an operation."

"Whoa." I squeezed Jenn's arm. "Let the doctor explain."

"Sorry, doc," Jenn said.

"It's fine, Jenn. Now Polly, take a look here…"

The doctor proceeded to explain to me that Little Bit had ingested something that was now causing a serious obstruction and pointed to a section of the intestinal tract where the blockage could clearly be seen.

"What do you think it is?"

"There's no telling from the x-ray. But I was able to palpate it and there's no way it's going to move. He's also severely dehydrated. I would say this happened at least two or three days ago. At this point the best thing is for me to go in and cut out the obstruction."

"Whatever you think best Dr. Jim. Miss Teasdale has already given me the go-ahead to do what's necessary."

"Good. Then I'm going to get him on some fluids right now, and start prepping him for the operation."

"How long will it take?" Jenn asked.

The doctor shook his head. "Depends what's in there, how badly it's stuck, has it perforated the intestinal wall…. We could be done in an hour or so, or it could be several hours. There's no need for you to wait. I'll call you as soon as I'm done."

Jenn and I looked at each other. "I'd rather stay," she said.

"Me, too," I agreed.

I made a quick call to Tyler and explained what had happened.

"Take your time, honey," he said. "Rooster's back with Tom but has sent him to rest. He's had a bad time and needs peace and quiet for a while, so there's nothing earth-shattering going on."

Relieved I wasn't being left out of anything important I reminded myself I had an obligation to my client. And I truly was worried about Little Bit. He was such a sweet cat. You could cradle him like a baby and he'd lay in your arms all day, purring like crazy. I resolved to concentrate on sending positive vibes into the Universe for his recovery.

"Polly, you guys can go back to room three. Dr. Jim will be with you in a few minutes."

The receptionist smiled at us encouragingly. I took that as a good sign. We'd been waiting a couple of hours for word of Little Bit. I'd spent that time alternating between visualizing the cat as well and happy, and rethinking the events at Welcome Home.

Doctor Jim looked serious as he entered. "Well, ladies, I have to say this is a first for me."

"Is he OK?" Jenn blurted out.

The doctor's expression relaxed. "He came through with flying colors. I'm going to keep him overnight to be on the safe side but you should be able to take him home in the morning."

"Then what do you mean by it's a first?" I asked.

From behind his back the doctor revealed a soggy, stringy thing. With finger and thumb from both hands he shook it out and held up a teeny, weeny lace thong.

"I'm not sure which one of you two this belongs to, but you might want to be a bit more careful where you leave such things." By now he was grinning broadly.

"It's not mine," Jenn said.

"And it's certainly not mine," I added.

"Well it surely can't belong to..." Dr. Jim began, looking aghast.

We all three gazed at the tiny undergarment, and a vision of the fifty-something Ardith Teasdale wearing it flashed into my mind; all five foot nothing and 300 pounds of her. It wasn't pretty.

Nine

"You haven't missed much," Rooster was reassuring me as he cut himself a hefty slice of pumpkin bread.

"If you cut another piece of that I'll get coffee," I said, pulling a couple of mugs from the cupboard. "And plenty of butter for me."

We sat across the table from each other and for several minutes munched and sipped quietly 'til Rooster broke the silence.

"Tom was jittery as a junebug and getting pretty angry when I picked him up. I figured he might be about to start getting flashbacks, so I had him take some meds and go lie down as soon as we got here."

"I'm not surprised, poor guy. An experience like this must be rife with triggers." PTSD, which nearly all our residents suffered with, is a cascade of symptoms— anxiety, anger, withdrawal among others, leading to flashbacks. It's a terrible thing to go through, in many ways because it's an invisible wound. Rooster was a rock at times like these and I felt a wave of gratitude that he'd come into our lives.

I bit into my pumpkin bread. "Was Tom able to tell you anything?"

"I let him be for now. I did get to have a few words with Felicks, though, and Tom is no longer at the top of the suspect list, though is still a person of interest."

"He still could have been the intended victim," I reminded Rooster.

"Could be, but I believe Felicks is concentrating now on the possibility that something was going on between Slattery and Ward Nesmith."

That was good to know. Rooster and Sheriff Wisniewski were good buddies and the top cop would sometimes drop inside information on Rooster. But why would he suspect there was link between the two men? I asked Rooster the question and he gave me a "Dunno."

I dunked my last piece of buttered bread in my coffee. Did you know butter stirred into coffee tastes delicious? Seriously, you should try it sometime. Grass-fed butter is best.

"By the way," I said, "where are Mom and Tyler?"

"Your mother's also taking a nap. She's hardly slept since the murder took place. And Tyler figured he'd check in at his office, said something about a new listing."

"How are we supposed to catch a killer if everyone disappears?"

Rooster gave me a "cut the nonsense look" and picked up a sheet of paper from the table.

"They went through the notes the residents wrote up and made a summary of relevant facts."

"Great. That's what we were working on when I got called away. Let me take a look." I snatched the paper and here's what I read:

- Early morning: Mom put the Santa outfit in the bathroom by the back door of the farmhouse. *Anyone who had access to the house could have known it was there. The general public did not have access.*

- The train was at the back of the farmhouse all day. *Various people worked on it throughout the day, and loaded the gifts in the carts. As far as we know, there was no-one with the train after Carl left at 6.20.*

- No-one recalls seeing Tom after about 5.30 when he said he was going to get ready for his Santa appearance. He reappeared when the body was found in the train at about 6.50. *Where was Tom during that time? Was Tom the intended victim? Who would have a motive to kill Tom?*

- Ward Nesmith was seen by several residents. Having been here a few times he was easily recognizable to them. No-one spoke to him or noticed if he was with anyone, except for Rooster who saw him with Slattery. (At that time, Rooster didn't know who Slattery was). *Why was Nesmith here? He must know he's not popular with any of us. What did he and Slattery have to talk about?*

- Chandler Slattery was unknown to all of us except Tyler, who did not notice him at the Open House. Several months ago Slattery made known his interest in buying Welcome Home but his offer was refused. *Was Slattery here merely to enjoy the festivities (unlikely) or to scope out the property (more likely). Why does the Sheriff have an interest in Slattery and Nesmith? Could they have been colluding to force us to sell?*

- From 6.20 on, all the residents, except Tom, claim to have been at their posts and are able to alibi each other. *Where was Tom? It's possible more than one person was involved in the murder, in which case some of the alibis could be suspect.*

"Jeez, the only thing this does is reinforce that we don't know anything!" I tossed the paper aside. "As I've said before, we need to find out from Tom what he was up to. And we should to talk to Nesmith; ask him about his relationship with the victim."

"And how do you propose to do that? You'd better not be thinking of approaching him on your own. He could be a killer."

"For goodness sakes, does nobody trust my judgement?"

Rooster's brows raised in quizzical fashion.

I huffed loudly. "Oh, alright. Maybe I have been a little hasty in the past, and maybe it did get me in a bit of trouble..."

A slight cough came from Rooster and he pursed his lips. *The man has a knack of getting his point across without saying a word.*

"OK, OK. I'll be a good girl. I'll ask Tyler to come with me."

"Not good enough. I want your pledge."

I grit my teeth and glared. Of course, it didn't make any difference. Once he set his mind to something Rooster was immovable, and I knew when I was beaten. So, meekly I raised my right hand and intoned, "I swear on the lives of all my furbabies that I will not approach Ward Nesmith alone. Satisfied?"

In response Rooster gave a barely perceptible nod.

"Well, if it meets with your approval," my voice was laced with sarcasm, "I'm off to see Dorcas."

Again with the slight nod so, feeling exasperated, I spun around and marched off.

Ten

Dorcas Phipps had moved her van to the side of the house where she'd hooked up to an electric outlet. Now that the yellow police tape had been removed I assumed Mom had told her it was OK to do so, but it made me wonder just how long she planned to hang around. I mean, if Mule's mother, Charlotte, combined with the full complement of Welcome Home's residents, hadn't found the pup by now, then I had to conclude this was a story with a sad ending.

It made me sick to think of all the dreadful things that might have happened so I shoved my thoughts aside and banged on the camper's door. Squeaky yips answered the noise – the two remaining puppies - though the door did not open.

"Over here!" As I was about to knock again I heard Dorcas call. She came from the back of the house with Charlotte on one of those extendable leads, and I could tell by the bits of twigs and leaves stuck on them that they must have been searching in the trees.

"We were raking about in case Mule got caught in some underbrush. If he dug down a bit it's possible he created a warm spot …"

The look on my face must have said all I was thinking. Dorcas shut up and dropped her gaze to the dog.

"I feel so guilty." A sob cracked her voice and in a wave of sympathy I put my arms around her.

Her reaction wasn't quite what I expected. She stiffened and pulled away.

"Sorry," she whispered. "Sorry. I, uh..." She shivered – not from the cold, I'm sure – before pulling herself together and giving me a thin smile. "I think the reality is setting in. He's gone isn't he?"

I pictured Mule's wrinkled bulldog puppy face. The black-rimmed eyes, the smudge above his mouth and the little brown spot perfectly placed on top of his head. I remembered how he reacted when I found him in the train; completely unruffled yet glad for attention. So young and already with so much personality. I wanted to lie to Dorcas and tell her there was still hope, but I figured that would be delaying the inevitable.

"I wish I could tell you everything will turn out fine. Truth is, it doesn't look that way." I paused, waiting for Dorcas to speak. When she didn't, I continued, gently. "Don't you think it's time for you to go home?"

In an instant, Dorcas's face tightened and her tone became waspish. "You're telling me to leave?"

"Well, no. I, uh, just thought you'd be happier in your own home." I glanced at the dog. "And it can't be easy living out of your van with Charlotte and the pups."

"So now you're telling me how to take care of my bulldogs?"

Duh? Aren't you the one who lost Mule? I didn't say that, of course, but my hackles were rising. We'd done

58

nothing but try and help the woman and now she was turning on us.

Perhaps sensing my ire, Dorcas suddenly deflated. *Good grief, the woman was a chameleon.*

"Polly, forgive me. Your family have been wonderful. And you're right, I should go home, at least then I'd probably get a good night's sleep; I'm not feeling very well at the moment."

I studied her face and noticed the sunken eyes and gray pallor to her skin.

"Look, Dorcas, you're no good to anybody if you don't take care of yourself."

She hesitated. "You're right. Do you mind, though, if I wait 'til the morning to leave? For now I just need to lie down."

"Sure. Is there anything I can get you?"

"No thanks. I'll be fine."

I watched her enter the van. The puppies tumbled excitedly around their mother, the show of happiness lifting my spirits. The feeling didn't last but a minute. As soon as I turned and took in the sight of the decorations around the house my good humor left me. So much effort had been put into creating our Christmas realm, and not a light had been turned on.

I wanted Christmas back. That meant I needed answers. Tom Ouelette might have some of those answers, so I squared my shoulders and strode to the barn to confront him.

The lower level of the barn was one large room with a kitchenette at the far side. Gerry and another guy were leaning against the counter, sodas in hand as they talked.

"What number is Tom's room?" I asked.

They showed no surprise at my abrupt question and the answer came back promptly, "Four."

I took the stairs two at a time and stopped in front of the door with a 4 on it. That's when I wavered. What if something I said or did sparked a flashback? I couldn't imagine Gerry would have let me come up here if there was any danger. Still, it might be prudent of me to enlist Rooster's help. Come to think of it, Rooster was likely to be pretty pissed if I approached Tom without him.

With hand fisted ready to knock, these thoughts raced through my mind, when the door slowly opened a few inches.

"Hayley?"

She put her finger to her lips and glanced back into the room, then slipped out, closing the door behind her.

"He's sleeping," she said.

"What are you doing here?" I knew I sounded suspicious but as I watched color rise in Hayley's face I knew my feelings were right.

Hayley cocked her head to the side. "Let's go somewhere private."

I followed her out of the barn and wordlessly we went to the farmhouse, where she had a room upstairs. I entered ahead of her and sat on the single chair and waited. Hayley stood, moving her weight from one foot to another then suddenly reached past me, grabbing a photograph from the nightstand and holding it out for me.

"You and Tom?" The picture was a selfie, a head shot of Hayley and Tom, cheek to cheek and grinning like sappy lovers.

"It started about three months ago," Hayley said. "I was an Army medic, and struggled with PTSD myself, so it's not unusual for the guys to talk to me about their problems. With Tom it turned into something different but we agreed it would be best to keep it quiet. On one hand I didn't want the others to feel they shouldn't talk to me, and then there were a few who had come on to me in the past, and I was concerned jealousy would raise its ugly head. I'd made it clear when I came here that I wasn't available to anyone, then Tom just, you know, happened."

Yeah, I could understand that.

"Listen, your relationship is none of my business so long as it doesn't interfere with anything else at Welcome Home."

"That's just the point." Hayley hung her head, then sat on the edge of the bed, hands clasping her knees. "Gerry found out."

"Is he one of the ones who made a pass at you?"

"Yeah. I didn't realize his feelings went so deep. I mean, it's not like I'm a raving beauty or anything, but the male to female ratio is definitely in my favor."

She was wrong about the beauty part. She wasn't one of those typical Hollywood "beauties," who've all been sculpted to look the same, but had soft features, wide-set eyes and a generous mouth. I could see why men would fall for her.

"Did things get nasty with Gerry?"

"He was more hurt than angry. The thing is, it made me realize I should never have allowed the relationship with Tom to get so far. That's why Tom was late for the Open House."

"I don't get it."

Hayley leaned closer. "He was with me. Here, in my room." She took a deep breath and straightened up again.

"Gerry confronted me earlier in the day; he'd seen Tom and I together. So later, when Tom found me alone, I told him it was over. He wouldn't accept that and followed me here when I tried to get away from him. We argued. Neither of us realized how late it was until we thought we heard shrill barking. It must have been the puppy, Mule. We looked out the window in time to see the train moving off. Tom sprinted downstairs, and you know the rest."

"Not quite," I said. "Why were you in his room just now?" I pretty much knew the answer already, but I wanted to hear it from her.

"He needed me."

I lifted my brows and gave my best piercing look.

Hayley returned it with a winsome smile. "And I'm in love with him."

I reassured Hayley everything would work out OK for her and Tom. I'd explain the situation to the others and let Rooster face Sheriff Wisniewski with the news, because it was obvious Tom had not informed him where he was when the murder took place.

Oh. A thought struck me. Was it possible Gerry was angry enough to want to kill Tom? Could he have killed Santa thinking it was his nemesis?

Eleven

Tyler and I were parked across the street from Ward Nesmith's home in a middle-class subdivision of cookie cutter houses. The kind of houses where you could open your bedroom window and shake hands with your neighbor, the places were so close together.

True to my word I was not going it alone with Nesmith. Tyler had suggested we ambush him at home – er, I should say "approach" him at home – rather than his office, on the assumption it would be harder for him to get away from us. We'd easily found his address online and arrived a little before we anticipated he'd get there. The idea was to ring the doorbell before he got settled.

"Shouldn't he be here by now? What if he decided to go out to dinner?" I fidgeted in my seat.

"Stop jumping to conclusions," Tyler said, "like Gerry being the killer."

Oh, yeah. When I told Tyler my fears about Gerry he pointed out that Gerry had been alibied by at least a dozen people because he was part of the choir. They'd been in the small barn doing a final run-through of some of the songs, then walked together to the stage to get in place for the switching on of the lights.

Talking of lights, it was getting very dusky and the street lights were coming on. An old SUV turned into the road and then into the Nesmith driveway. The garage doors opened and the vehicle disappeared inside.

"Here we go," Tyler said.

At the front door, the only nod to Christmas was a tired-looking wreath. The doorbell didn't work so Tyler banged hard with his gloved hand, but it wasn't Ward who stood before us when the door opened. A young boy politely inquired "Can I help you?" He seemed to have a slight speech impediment – it came out more like "Can I hep you?" - but before we had a chance to reply a younger girl pushed in front of him, saying, "Hi, I'm Glory." In her arm she carried a chubby, wrinkly puppy with a smudge on his mouth and a brown splodge on top of his head. "And this is Olaf," said Glory, trying to thrust him forward for our inspection.

My jaw practically dropped to my knees. I knew the little bulldog pup as Mule. What shocked me even more were the braces on the child's legs and the wheeled walker she was hanging on to.

Tyler's ability to recover was much faster than mine. "Hello, Glory," he said and, "Hi, Olaf," scratching the puppy's brown spot.

"Children, who is it?" The woman who came up behind the kids tapped the boy lightly on his shoulder. When he turned his face to her she began to sign and mouthed words to him. In response, he bent down and took the puppy from the girl, saying in his stilted way, "Give me Olaf, Glory." *Good grief. The boy was deaf.*

The woman turned her attention to us and smiled warmly. I liked her instantly, which made me feel awkward about being there. Tyler, thankfully, was still in command of his feelings.

"We're here to see Ward," he said.

"Oh, of course. I didn't know he was expecting anyone. Come in, come in. You'll freeze out there." We stepped inside. "Ward got home only a few minutes ago, he's putting his slippers on. I'll go and tell him you're here. Oh, I don't know your names."

"It's alright, Merry. I'm here."

Ward Nesmith stood on the far side of the room. My first impression was that he looked defeated, but when Glory called out, "Daddy, Daddy," and hurried to him as fast as her braces and walker would take her, his whole being changed. He caught her in his arms and twirled around.

"How is my beautiful princess?"

Glory laughed with glee, and beside me Merry spoke in a low voice. "He gets so tired and he works so hard, but the children always make him feel better."

On the contrary, I was now feeling decidedly glum. Had we walked onto the set of "A Christmas Carol?" The Nesmith's were beginning to look like Bob Cratchit and his wife, with Glory playing the part of Tiny Tim. Did that make me Scrooge?

Cratchit, uh, I mean Nesmith, hugged his son then turned to his wife. "I think a little hot chocolate would be nice, my dear. The children can help you."

She understood his veiled request for privacy and ushered the kids away with promises of extra marshmallows.

Nesmith's expression turned suspicious. "What are you doing here?"

Again, Tyler took the lead. "I'm truly sorry we burst in on your family this way. I hope you understand we're here on behalf of the veterans at Welcome Home. This murder is jeopardizing their welfare. We heard recently that you knew Chandler Slattery and are hoping you can answer a few questions."

Delicately put, my wonderful guy.

"Like did I kill the man?" Nesmith wasn't being at all delicate.

I finally found my voice. "Did you?"

He sighed heavily. "You'd better sit down."

We dropped onto a small loveseat and waited while Nesmith appeared to gather his thoughts. I took the time to look around at the worn furniture and fraying carpet. In spite of the furnishings having seen better days, the room had a cozy, welcoming feel. Homemade Christmas ornaments decked the mantel where a fire was burning. In the corner a live spruce tree was hung with glass balls and strings of popcorn, and fresh cut holly had been arranged in vases.

Something touched my foot. I looked down and there was Mule – or should I say, Olaf – attacking my bootlaces. I picked him up and hugged him, reveling in his warmth and his puppy breath, and ridiculously grateful he was alive.

"Perhaps we could start with him," I said to Nesmith.

"Let me tell it my way," he said. And he did.

"Chandler Slattery approached me right after I did the first inspection at Welcome Home. He wanted me to find reasons to stop construction on the barns, and offered me a lot of money to do it."

"So that's why you forced us to make changes. You were trying to get us to give up!"

Keeping his tone even but firm, Nesmith replied. "No. Those changes were to bring the construction up to code, necessary for the safety of the residents. Something the previous inspector should have made sure of. And as it happens, I turned Slattery down flat. Much as the money was tempting, I am a man of principal and never wished to put the veterans at risk of losing their homes."

"Well you did," I snapped.

Nesmith started. "They were still able to live there while changes were made."

"True enough. But their housing benefits were withheld. It was lucky we had enough funds in reserve to keep going."

He looked stricken. "I'm sorry. I guess I could have handled things better."

I wasn't sure how to respond to that, but I didn't have to. Merry Nesmith stepped into the room.

"I need to say something." Directing her attention to her husband she added, "The kids are making the hot chocolate." Then to Tyler and me she said, "I wanted to listen. I know who you are, Polly. Ward talked a lot about your veterans' home and he was very impressed with what you were doing. I also know my husband will never defend himself when it comes to his job..."

"Merry," Ward stopped her. "Don't make excuses."

Tenderly she touched the back of her hand to his cheek. "Alright, no excuses, but I want them to know there was a reason you were struggling with work at that time."

Talking again to us she continued. "Glory was being fitted for her leg braces and it wasn't going well. She has cerebral palsy, caused by her mother violently and repeatedly shaking her as a baby. The leg braces gave her the chance to have some independence and a little normality in her life. Without them she'd be confined to a wheelchair. You can imagine how stressful it was for us.

"The situation with Slattery didn't help. It wasn't as simple as Ward implied. The man kept badgering him, even threatened his job. Honestly, we were scared. Then when I saw that dreadful man at the Christmas event, and he had the nerve to plague Ward again, well, I could have killed him myself." In an aside she added, "I didn't."

"Tell me," Tyler asked, "did either of you see Slattery with anyone else, or did he say anything to suggest he could be in danger?"

"We were there for a fun family night out," Ward said. "After I brushed him off we stayed as far from him as possible."

"I don't know if it helps," Merry absent mindedly toyed with a cross around her neck, "but I did hear a rumor that Slattery's wife was going to divorce him. Apparently, he was something of a ladies' man and she'd had enough."

"You think his wife killed him?" I asked.

"I'm not sure what I think. She's the one who had the money, I'm told, and I don't suppose he'd want to give that up."

"But he had a successful business; money wouldn't be an issue."

"Oh, it was." Ward said. "His company was in trouble, that's why he was so desperate to get your property cheap."

Wow. This visit was turning out to be quite a revelation.

All this time, Mule/Olaf had been dozing on his back in my lap. I tickled his tummy, his legs twitched and he made sleepy squeaking noises. All eyes were drawn to the display of cuteness.

"We have to deal with this," I said.

Merry and Ward exchanged anxious glances. It was Merry who spoke.

"We knew it couldn't last. When Glory saw the pups at the Open House, she instantly fell in love. We tried to explain we couldn't afford a puppy but her heart had been stolen. It wasn't so different to the way Ward and I felt when we first saw Robby and Glory." She looked lovingly at her husband.

"We were devastated when we found out we couldn't have children, and the idea of adoption didn't appeal at all. Then one of our church members who fosters special needs kids brought a young boy to the Christmas Eve service: it was love at first sight. That was five years ago. Same thing with Glory. We've loved her now for a year; and Robby adores his little sister." She bit her lip. "That's why he took the puppy for her."

Once again I was stuck for words, and this time so was Tyler.

Wouldn't you know, it was at that awkward time the children came back with a tray of hot chocolate and cookies. Glory's face lit up at the sight of the puppy and she came over to me and kissed his nose, ever so softly. Robby followed and offered the tray.

"You have to eat a cookie. Me and Robby helped Mommy make them, then we decorated them. You should have that one," Glory nudged a cookie toward me. "I did that one, it's a Christmas tree."

She was so proud of herself. Dutifully I took a bite. "It's delicious." *Really, it was.*

"Children," I heard Merry's voice, "there's something we have to talk about." Her hands flew as she signed to Robby.

"Oh... uh..." I almost choked on my cookie. I knew she was going to say the puppy had to be returned and I wasn't at all sure that was the thing to do. "Why don't we talk about this later? We can work something out."

Ward's brow wrinkled. "The kids have to learn to do the right thing."

"I get that, I do. All I'm saying is, let's take some time to figure out exactly what the right thing is."

"Polly, I appreciate what you're trying to do, but we can't afford to take care…"

"Stop right there." I waved my hand before he said something in front of Glory and Robby. "Please give me a chance to think of something."

He opened his mouth to reply when Merry took his hand. "Ward. Please."

Under his wife's pleading look, Ward caved. But only a little.

"We'll take the puppy to the rescue place in the morning."

"Come to Welcome Home. Dorcas Phipps is still there with the pup's mother. If you can be there about ten I'll make sure she's available."

Glory wrinkled her face in puzzlement. "Is Olaf going to see his mommy?"

"Yes, darling," Merry said.

"Oh, goodie." She beamed. "You'll like that, won't you Olaf?"

A few minutes later Tyler and I crossed the road and got in the car. Glory had insisted we finish our cookies and hot chocolate, then both kids hugged us goodbye as if we were their favorite aunt and uncle.

"Do you feel as humbled as I do?" I asked.

"Probably more," Tyler said.

"We had Ward pegged completely wrong. What a lovely family they are."

Tyler nodded. "What are you going to do about Mule?"

"Olaf," I corrected. "I have absolutely no idea."

Twelve

Something was tickling my nose. In my half-awake state I swatted at it and felt fur. Amber! My little calico. Sometimes she likes to stick her nose in my ear or chew my hair; either way she won't stop 'til I get up. I twisted as best I could with two other cats and three dogs on the bed with me, to look at the clock. Seven.

I pushed my furkids aside. Time to get up. I wanted to be out at the farm to talk to Dorcas before the Nesmiths arrived.

Tyler had driven me back to the farmhouse last night where I'd found Dorcas in her camper. When I told her Mule was safe and would be back at ten in the morning she burst into tears and sank to the floor. Alarmed, I helped her onto the bed. She looked pretty ragged but insisted she was OK.

"I've been so worried, I haven't been sleeping."

"Let me bring you some chamomile tea," I said. "That always helps me."

It wasn't the right time to discuss Mule's future, so I gathered up the dogs and came back to my little house in town. The cats were delighted to have me back as usual. On the few occasions I stay with Mom I take them with me but this time, with all the noise and activity going on, I decided they'd be happier at home. Still, they missed the company so I skipped my morning coffee to give the three of them some extra cuddling before rushing out again with Vinny, Coco and Angel.

A couple of the veterans were walking dogs as I pulled into Welcome Home, and Rooster was leaning against the porch railings, coffee mug in hand, keeping an eye on Elaine as she went about her morning business. I caught a whiff of the strong brew as I went up the steps and decided I'd better fuel myself with some caffeine before I tackled Dorcas.

There was always a pot of coffee on in the kitchen. The rule was whoever poured the last cup started the next pot. Helping myself to a couple of cookies as well I stood munching and nibbling, looking out the back window. A beautiful red cardinal landed on a branch and began preening. How nice, I thought, to have at least one splash of color when everything else seemed so drab.

Not just one, I realized as my attention was drawn to a stirring deeper in the trees where I caught a flash of blue. What was it? One of the dogs?

Setting my nearly empty cup down I went out the back door and headed toward the disturbance. Now I could tell it was someone on hands and knees who appeared to be digging. Or were they hacking at tree roots?

My approach was pretty noisy; I had no reason for stealth. The figure suddenly stiffened and straightened, then Dorcas Phipps turned her head to look at me.

"What on earth are you doing?" I asked, gazing at the butcher's knife in her hand and stupidly wondering if she was cutting greens for Christmas decorations. The look of guilt I then noted on her face dispelled that notion, and in rapid succession other thoughts fired in my brain and I knew I was facing a killer.

Dorcas stood and squared off in front of me, knife pointing my way.

I tried to stay calm and calculate my chances if I ran. We were about the same height, but would my fear give me an edge over her compulsion to fight? *Talk her down*, I told myself. *Isn't that what you're supposed to do?*

"Killing me won't help, Dorcas. You'll never get away with it."

She took a step toward me and I stepped back. "I must say, it was clever of you to dress the body in the Santa suit. That is what you did, isn't it? I can admire that kind of fast-thinking because I'm sure you didn't plan to kill Slattery, did you?"

"He hurt me. He'd said he loved me and wanted to be with me, but it was all a lie. When I confronted him he laughed. Do you believe that? He laughed at me, and what do you think I did? I *begged* him. I made a bigger fool of myself than I already had and I begged him to leave his wife and be with me. Then he laughed even harder and it made me so angry," now she was sobbing.

"I wasn't thinking. I don't even remember picking the stone up but there it was in my hand and I hit him. It made a soft thudding noise and he gave me a look of such surprise, then he crumpled. I looked at the stone and it was a Santa head: red hat, white whiskers and chubby red cheeks. It looked at me as if it was accusing me and I just wanted to get rid of it, so I threw it as far away as I could, into the trees. But it reminded me I'd seen a Santa suit in the bathroom when I'd gone in there earlier, and it gave me an idea."

"You dressed Slattery in the suit. That was a heck of a risk, though. Tom was supposed to be getting ready by then, he could have turned up at any moment."

"Maybe that wasn't the best idea. Believe it or not, you don't think straight when you've just killed your lover." She laughed maniacally. *Oh, Lord, she was losing it.* "I thought I was buying time to distance myself from what happened."

"Did you know then that Mule was missing?" In spite of being in danger I was still trying to piece together all the facts.

Dorcas managed to look contrite. "I didn't realize 'til after. That's when I began to be glad Chandler was dead. Because of him I'd left the dogs unattended, otherwise Mule would be safe."

"He is safe now, Dorcas." I kept my voice low. "He'll be here very soon. Don't you want to see him?"

"Of course I do," she snapped. "But I have to take care of you first," and she held the knife out, taking another step nearer.

OK, the talking thing wasn't working; it was time to run. I spun quickly, only to snag my foot on a tangle of dead vines. I went down on my side, my foot twisting beneath me and a searing pain shot through my ankle. I tried to shake free but the vine might as well have been nylon filament, it wouldn't give.

I looked up. Dorcas was almost on me and from somewhere nearby I heard high-pitched yips and a voice yelling, "Hey." Dorcas hesitated, looking away in confusion, then a body hurled past me and charged into her, knocking her to the ground. The knife flew from her grasp and embedded itself in the trunk of an Eastern White Pine.

You probably think it was Tyler who saved me, seeing as it's usually his role. This time, however, it was Ward Nesmith. Who knew he could move like a linebacker?

The Nesmiths had arrived and parked beside Dorcas's camper van. Ward knocked and the dogs made noise. Mule/Olaf got excited. Realizing Dorcas was not there, Merry suggested they move away so the puppy would calm down and they walked behind the house. It was the pups continued yapping that distracted Dorcas from knifing me, and it was Robby who saw something was wrong. He nudged his dad and Ward sprinted into action.

We were all still behind the farmhouse. Rooster and a couple of the other guys had taken hold of Dorcas, who had completely deflated. Mom was fussing over my ankle, telling me an ambulance was on the way. Merry had sent the children closer to the trees where they were playing with Mule and his siblings, and their mother, who had been released from the camper. Ward was sitting next to me on the back stairs while Merry dabbed peroxide on a couple of scratches he'd got on his face.

"I see my knight in shining armor status has been challenged." Tyler had walked up unnoticed. His gaze went from me to Ward, then he held out his hand. "And all I can say is, thank you."

Ward grasped the hand and both men shook solemnly. Soon after, Sheriff Wisniewski arrived, which gave me the opportunity to say we'd solved his case for him. I have to give him credit, he took it well, but did say he'd learned of the affair between Dorcas and the victim and had been taking a closer look at her.

"When it came to the ladies," the Sheriff said, "Slattery was a busy boy."

"I feel sorry for Dorcas," I said.

"I don't," Mom snapped.

"She's what, fortyish? Never married. Her life has revolved around her beloved bulldogs. She's not someone men pay attention to, then suddenly there's this charismatic guy who sweeps her off her feet. She fell big time and he turned out to be scum."

"What will happen to her dogs now?" Merry asked.

"There are other people involved with the rescue. They'll be taken care of, and I'm quite sure there won't be any problem now with adopting Mule."

"Oh, Polly," Merry sighed. "There's still a problem with the cost."

"We have an idea for that," Mom said. "Polly and I talked last night. We can always use extra help around here and we thought the kids could come over, say a couple of times a month, and do a few chores in exchange for dog food and supplies."

Ward shook his head. "There are still vet bills and other expenses…"

"Come on hon," Merry gave his shoulder a squeeze, "we can work it out. I can help, too, and…"

"Mom! Mom!" Glory's urgent call interrupted. "Look what Olaf found."

Merry hurried to the children and took something from her child. She went quite still, staring at it, then called back to us. "It's a gnome's head."

Olaf, formerly known as Mule, had found the head in a hole under a tree root. We guessed that when Dorcas tossed the thing it must have hit a branch, bounced back and rolled into its hiding place. Remarkably, it hadn't broken. All the time Dorcas claimed to be searching in the trees for the puppy she'd been looking to find the gnome head and destroy it, fearful her fingerprints were on it. After being slobbered on by dogs and handled by the kids, there was little likelihood of that now. Good thing she'd confessed.

I felt kind of stupid that I hadn't suspected Dorcas. Think of it. She was so adamant about staying close to the scene of the crime, but it was to follow the murder investigation, not to find a lost puppy. Then when she fell apart telling me how guilty she felt, she was talking about the murder, and I assumed it was about losing Olaf.

Oh, well. Things turned out alright in the end.

Thirteen

Vinny looked adorable in his elf outfit, only no-one in the audience could see it because he was refusing to come on stage. It had been set up as Santa's workshop and Vinny, followed by Coco (looking equally adorable, I must say), were supposed to enter carrying gifts.

In a low voice I did my best to coax Vinny. It wasn't that he was unwilling, he just got distracted easily and at the moment was showing more interest in the leg of a table holding props. In an effort to spur him on, Tyler tossed the gift onstage and gave Vinny a shove. In return Vinny sniffed his rear and the crowd, finally able to see him, shouted encouragement.

"Vinny," I whispered. "Chicken," and showed him a piece of meat tucked in my hand. I guess he didn't see it, but Coco certainly did. She burst onto the stage and tore around in circles then jumped up and down trying to get my attention. In an attempt to go on with the show I signaled Tyler to let Angel go. She stepped onto the stage and in a couple of deft moves with her paw pulled off her reindeer antlers and harness, then lay on her stomach daring me to try and put them back on.

The good thing is the audience was loving it. And after this fiasco maybe Mom wouldn't make me do anything next year.

While people were still cheering I gathered my mutts and made my escape to the house. At the porch I stopped and looked out at the brightly lit trees, the Santa train, reindeer, snowmen and yes, gnome elves. So many people had come back even after the tragedy of the week before and there were lots of familiar faces, friends old and new.

The Nesmiths were among them, but without Olaf who was safe at home. We'd already put the kids to work, Robby helping Tyler with props for the show, and Glory was designated to add sprinkles to the cookies as Scott and Lou baked them.

This was the part of Christmas I loved best. People embracing the giving spirit. Some, like our veterans and volunteers, gave their time and expertise to create enjoyment and raise funds for our shelter. Others gave their support through donations or showed it just by turning up at our events and making our efforts worthwhile.

For a few moments more I watched the smiling faces and my heart swelled with joy. A voice from the crowd called out, "Merry Christmas, Polly," and was soon joined by a chorus of others. I couldn't tell who it was, but I raised my hand and waved madly, "Merry Christmas everyone," as the choir began to sing, "Joy to the World."

Go here to get a **FREE** short story from Liz, and become part of the In Crowd:

http://lizdodwell.com/signup/

Get other books in the Polly Parrett series:

Doggone Christmas
The Christmas Kitten
Bird Brain
Seeing Red

Find all of Liz's stories here.

http://lizdodwell.com/books/

Are you a coloring enthusiast? Here's where you'll find Liz's coloring books:

http://www.mix-booksonline.com/category/coloring-books

Liz Dodwell

...devotes her time to writing and publishing from the home she shares with husband, Alex and a host of rescued dogs and cats, collectively known as "the kids." She will tell you, "I gladly suffer the luxury of working from home where I'm with my 'kids,' can toss in a load of laundry in between plotting, writing, editing and general office work while still in my PJs. I love what I do and know how lucky I am to be able to do it. Oh, and if you asked me what my hobbies are, I'd probably say reading murder mysteries, drinking champagne, romantic dinners with my husband and yodeling (just joking about that last one)."

Printed in the USA
CPSIA information can be obtained
at www.ICGtesting.com
LVHW051938011224
798044LV00010B/973